Kitsuneko

A COMPANION NOVELLA TO

THE REALMS BEYOND THE RAINBOW

❋ ❋ ❋ ❋

C. S. Johnson

Copyright © 2019 by C. S. Johnson.

1st Edition.

ISBN ebook: 978-1-948464-33-8

ISBN Paperback: 978-1-948464-34-5

THE REALMS BEYOND THE RAINBOW

This is for my own sweet little princess. I thank God every day that he gave you to me.

This book is also for my dear friend, Laura, a unicorn princess if I ever met one. Unicorns might be rare, but good friends like you are even more so.

THE REALMS BEYOND THE RAINBOW

To Get *Awakening* (A Special Christmas Episode of The *Starlight Chronicles*) as a bonus for picking up this book,

Click Here

Or Download It At:
https://www.csjohnson.me/awakening

THE REALMS BEYOND THE RAINBOW

CHAPTER ONE

I look in the mirror carefully, scrutinizing the smallest details of the face before me. It is the face of a beautiful young woman, serene and striking all at once. I study the rosy cheeks, still youthfully plump while they start to hint at adulthood, while golden hair falls to either side, sweeping long past the pointed chin. My focus fastens onto the nose in wonderment, mesmerized by the size of the little bump that turns up at its end. I press down on it with my finger, and it shrinks, ever so slightly, in size.

Finally, my gaze travels to see the two large, slanted eyes staring back at me; the misty green twinkles, simultaneously bewildered and cautious.

The eyes are mine, even if the rest of the face is not.

Of all the different kinds of changelings, the kitsunefolk are the only ones whose eyes refuse to change. I doubt this is anything but by design; my kinfolk are known for their inner stubbornness as much as they are known for their outward flexibility. Add in the catblood, and that's me.

I am a changeling from the Honeyspice Lands, a kitsune-neko, and that's all. That is my only role to play in the grand kingdom of Toulacoeur, and so much so, that's what they named me.

I am Kitsuneko, slave of King Dario and his wife, Queen Arianna, their full-time substitute for their daughter, Princess Cari.

I smile into the mirror, and the face of Princess Cari smiles back at me.

"Perfect," I whisper. "You look just like her."

Or at least, I look like what most people think Princess Cari would look like, if she hadn't been kidnapped seventeen years ago.

"Well, where is she? Isn't she ready yet?"

The anxious voice of the queen cuts through my concentration; my pointed, black-tipped ears, the ears of a fox-cat changeling, suddenly shoot out of either side of my head, instinctively twitching and shuddering. I watch with remorse, and only a little bit of prideful cheer, as the blonde hair of the princess changes to my usual shade of reddish brown.

I touch the ears and rub them, praying to the god of Toulacoeur for comfort. I don't know if he hears me, but there is an unspeakable sense of peace that settles around me. Calm once more, my ears slip back into my head, and I am able to hold my transformation.

A small sigh escapes me. I've always been a good changeling—my very life and its quality depends on it, after all—but no matter my level of skill or the amount of time I practice, there are always some moments I can't control it, especially when I am alone.

Perhaps after all the time I have spent covering up, I owe it to myself to figure out just who it is I am erasing.

Back in the mirror, the princess's shapely lips curve into a dark, wry smile as my ears begin to slip back into Cari's crown of golden locks. *Or perhaps it is good that the king and queen don't allow me to be alone very often then, hmm?*

It's not as if I am the only changeling in the world able to mimic Princess Cari's likeness; I was just the most convenient one around when they conscripted me into service, and I will be quickly disposed of if I become inconvenient.

Almost as if they can hear my thoughts, the door swings open. I suck in my breath and squeeze my eyes shut, allowing myself one last second to myself, before facing the inevitable.

"Kitty?"

My breath leaves me in one long exhale, and I almost giggle at my happy turn of fate. "Lights above, Kiro, I thought you were your mother."

"You mean 'our mother,' don't you?" My pretend brother's teasing tone is light, but I know just from looking at him that despite his smile, he is struggling just as much as I am.

His eyes narrow he looks around my room.

"No one else is here," I tell him, and I can see this is what he wants to hear. His shoulders relax, if only momentarily.

We are children of the king and queen, and our privacy is as rare to us as gold to the poorest of the poor.

"I guess there are no festivities today, other than dancing and eating? I can't imagine you'd be allowed to wear that otherwise," I say, pointing to his spiderfly silk shirt and the rich brocade of his vest as I try lightening his mood a little more.

"Of course not. The king and queen never bother themselves with what I want, not even at my birthday ball."

I reach over and pull him into what is supposed to be a quick hug. "It'll be fine in the end. It's only for one night, after all. We can go on one of our secret adventures tomorrow, if that will make you feel better."

For the past several years, Kiro and I have indulged ourselves in different outings, from exploring the hidden rooms of the palace, to secret picnics—even sneaking into the city in disguise. We aren't able to do them very often, not without risking anger from the king and queen or discovery by the guards or the citizens. But I feel it is worth the hazard, if it will only make Kiro happy.

Kiro says nothing as he continues to embrace me.

My breath catches in my throat. It doesn't matter how many times he's held me before, I am always surprised at Kiro's gentleness. With his broad shoulders and narrow hips, Kiro is a perfect mirror to the king and his legacy as a legendary warrior. He is much taller than me, even with the illusion of Cari's height. His hair is the color of warm moonlight, while his blue eyes, bright with intelligence and laughter, gaze past the barriers of our world.

While I have learned beside him or followed behind him nearly all my life, Kiro has always been my best friend and only confidante. I know him better than I even know myself. He is not the only one who knows I am not really his sister, but he is the only one who never held it against me. Every kindness he has ever shown me, I have harbored in my memory, using that collection as a bulwark to keep back the sad weariness of his mother's depression or his father's oppressive neglect.

I wonder at how well I fit in his arms, even if it is no wonder to me that I am in love with him.

At that thought, I pull back from him, more than a little reluctantly. He is still nervous, and I suppose I can't blame him.

Tonight is the night of his twentieth birthday ball. Kiro is now of age to inherit the kingdom, should the king abdicate, or if something else should happen. He is the future, and the future is secure; everyone in the kingdom is excited for him.

Everyone, of course, except me.

But just as I pretend to be his older sister, I put on a false smile and pretend to be happy for him tonight.

I owe him too much to want to tell him the truth.

"Mother wants to know if you're ready for tonight, if you haven't already heard," Kiro says. This time, his voice is more restrained, and I know it's time to concern ourselves with our duties.

He has always been a good son, and I have always done my best to fulfill my duty, too.

"Of course," I agreed, switching my voice to mimic the queen's accent and standing up straighter. "I was just finishing up. You know, making sure everything's in the right place."

"Unless my sister ever returns to Toulacoeur, we'll never know what's supposed to be the right place." He scoffs. "I like you better when it's *really* you, Kitty."

My heart both leaps and falls at his moment of honesty, and I swallow hard, knowing it will be even more difficult for me to make it through the night.

"I could look like you, if you think that would be better," I say, already reworking my face to look like his. It takes me only a few seconds to transform my face perfectly into his, other than the eyes, and when I scowl at him in play, he finally laughs.

"Cari's face is better suited to your dress than mine," Kiro says. "Remind me to never make you mad."

"Yes, somehow I don't think the king's guards would let you forget it if they saw you in this," I agree. The gown the queen had sent up earlier was very beautiful; it was a fine, silvery gray, like a raincloud about to burst. The long sleeves and square neckline, together with the high waist, made me feel taller as much as it made me look older. I tugged at the long skirt, showing off its fullness. I let my face resume its impression of Cari as I playfully twirl around. "Still, it's very lovely. I think it's a good sign that the silk trade agreements are still going strong among the realms, right?"

When I look up, I see Kiro is staring intently at me, in such a way that stops my heart as much as it makes it beat faster.

Before I can say anything—before I can breathe properly again—he frowns and nods. "You'll pass for Cari, as usual."

"No need to say it so sullenly," I say. "I like to think my talent has improved over the years."

"It needed to, with all your growth spurts." Kiro slips around me, grabbing my hand and leading me into another spin. "You're not sporting a tail this time, are you?"

THE REALMS BEYOND THE RAINBOW

"No." I grab at the back of the gown they'd sent me, the smoothness of its finery easily making my hands slip around my backside. There is no tail, fortunately, and I hate how relieved I feel. I whirl around so Kiro can't see, but as I turn, in that second, I catch his gaze lingering on my body, and I blush. The heat on my cheeks burns even more as Kiro clears his throat.

"Well, that's good," he says. "I remember when that happened at your last birthday, the queen spent a good two weeks in her bed while the king just raged whenever someone mentioned your 'foolish prank.'"

I don't say anything. I do not want to remind him of the days following that episode. After the king had chastised me, threatening me with whippings and even imprisonment, I'd been scared to leave my room. Two days had passed as I starved, before Kiro had shown up at my door with an armful of pilfered treats from the kitchen.

The kingdom is in a tenuous enough position. Rumors of Cari's kidnapping have never fully disappeared; I know there is speculation among the population that I am an imposter, a child the king and queen adopted to take Cari's place.

It isn't the truth, but it is too close for comfort.

I had been too young to remember everything myself, only that the princess's disappearance was upsetting and dangerous; of course, at the time, I'd only just arrived at the palace myself. I'd been a gift for the king and queen from an ambassador from the Honeyspice Lands, one who claimed he'd found me as a stowaway in one of his spice warehouses. I was three years old at the time, and my changeling abilities were just starting to allow me to look fully human.

Even all these years later, things are still bad enough, with the queen's health failing drastically, and the other realms starting to doubt the unity Toulacoeur's legacy offered. Kiro's birthday today was a mark in securing the kingdom's rule, even if the question of its protection remained uncertain.

"Well, let's go and get this over with." Kiro puts his hand on my arm. The strength I feel in him is thoughtfully restrained, and I lean into his softness. We stand there together, and it is only when I notice that he hasn't moved that I tug on his sleeve.

"Your mother—*our* mother—is waiting," I say.

He still doesn't move, and then he looks at me again. His blue eyes are mesmerizing; a second later, all the work I'd put into looking like Princess Cari is undone. My auburn hair overtakes the golden locks, the white lines that outline my eyes strike out like silver, and my pointed ears slip out once more. My cheeks are full of fire as I realize what's happened, and I try to pull back, embarrassed.

"No. Kitty, wait." Kiro doesn't let me move. The way he speaks my name is a symphony, his voice full of a richness and beauty that instantly captivates me, and I am lost as I stare back at him.

He brushes a strand of my hair away from my eyes. "I know it's the wrong time to tell you this … but … I … "

He steps closer and begins to lean toward me, bringing his mouth closer to mine. I feel the tremor of the earth inside of me as I realize he is going to kiss me, and there is nothing in me, not even my sense of duty, that will move to stop him.

I want him to kiss me, too.

My eyes close as my heart thunders between my ears, and I taste his breath as it mingles with mine.

Our lips are just about to touch as the hardened voice of Queen Arianna screeches between us.

"Kitsuneko, by all that is bright, where *are* you? The procession is leaving the castle!"

My eyes shoot open, and my trembling body jerks back out of Kiro's reach. The queen's anger is a weapon, a sword that remains sharp by its rare use more than its refining. Her voice summons back my common sense, reminding me more forcefully than ever I am only alive at her good will.

The absolutely last thing she would want is to find out I am in love with Kiro. That would be too inconvenient, not just for her, but for everyone else in the kingdom.

"I'm coming," I holler back, still blushing furiously but desperate to correct my outward features.

THE REALMS BEYOND THE RAINBOW

Kiro is surprised as much as I am, but thanks to his years training in the king's guard, he is able to hide it better. If I did not know him so well, I would have missed the nervous, angry way he ran his hand through his hair.

The door opens, and one of the queen's handmaidens, Juni, comes in. She really should be called a "hand-matron," considering her old age. In many ways, she is like the queen's mother, having been her nursemaid and later her first official handmaiden.

But despite her closeness to the queen, I like Juni. She is the one who calls me "Honeyspice," and just like Kiro calling me "Kitty," I feel a special bond with her because of it. She serves as a mother-figure to me, especially when the queen is too distraught to even look my way. Juni has watched over me and Kiro when, in our younger days, we would run through the palace gardens or go riding throughout Toulacoeur's capital, Auralis. Even then, I knew her softness as much as her sternness, and I was comforted that there was never one without an inkling of the other.

"Oh, Honeyspice," she coos, easily pushing past Kiro as she begins to paw at my gown. "You need to get moving. My Ari's fretting."

I nod frantically. "I was—"

"Just getting me to make sure she was all set," Kiro interrupts. "I'll go and tell Mother she doesn't need to worry so."

"Bangs, please," Juni orders me, parting my now-golden hair off to the side. I shorten the front to please her before she turns to give Kiro a skeptical smile. "I've been telling her that for years, Highness, and there's no point in pretending it helps. She's looking for a white unicorn to come riding over the horizon, and she won't be satisfied until she sees him again."

"True enough," Kiro agrees. He turns to me, his eyes still blazing with intensity. "We'll finish our conversation later."

I say nothing, only nodding and giving him an awkward half-smile as he leaves my room. My tongue is too thick and my pride is too scared to say anything else.

Juni distracts me at once, tugging on the train of my dress and checking the fit of my bodice.

"You need to be an inch taller," she says. "Cari is twenty-two now. She's past full-grown, I would imagine."

There's a sadness in her voice that carries over into my own heart. Princess Cari has grown up, assuming she survived, without her mother or her father and without her brother. There was no way to know what kind of life she'd lived since she'd been lost.

I am grateful I am at least able to have Kiro, though I wonder, as I think of how sure I'd been that he wanted to kiss me, how much longer my time with him will be.

Kiro and I will never be able to be together. He is a prince, and I am a slave.

"One last thing, and you'll be ready," Juni says. "Ari told me to make sure you wear Kleon's tiara."

"The Unicorn tiara?"

Juni nods firmly, trying to reassure my uncertainty. "Yes, Honeyspice," she says softly. "Tonight's an important night."

"I know." I swallow hard and try to look happy as Juni goes over to my jewelry cabinets and pulls out a chatelaine of keys. "Kiro's birthday is always fun for the kingdom to celebrate. I am sure now that he is old enough to take the throne, the people will be extra enthusiastic."

"That's not all we'll be celebrating tonight." Juni turns the key and unlocks the drawer, pulling out the Unicorn tiara.

I've only worn it once before, on Cari's twentieth birthday celebration two years before. It is the crown of the Unicorn's Keeper, a duty which has been passed down from daughter to daughter since the Seven Realms of the Rainbow was united by the first king, eleven generations before. He was the one who conquered all the realms with the blessing of Kleon the Unicorn, and from that point on, the seven realms have been at peace.

THE REALMS BEYOND THE RAINBOW

I gulp as Juni places the tiara on my head. I look back in the mirror, wondering at the pearls and diamonds that are expertly knotted into the white gold, before pulls it up into the twisted horn in its center. At its crest is a large ruby. The Shadowcavern dwarves, experts in mining, had likely provided it to King Dario at his request.

Not too many other people know it is supposed to be a red diamond, and that it had been lost along with the princess.

"You look beautiful," Juni whispers as she steps back from me. "You're doing Princess Cari proud, God give her soul peace."

"You don't think she's dead, do you?"

"Honestly? I don't know what to think." She sighs. "So I pray. I hope. But I don't know. I can only trust." Her wrinkled hands clasp together, and I can see she is upset. She likely didn't mean to comment so darkly on the princess' fate.

"I try to do the same," I say, and at my confession, she relaxes.

"I pray for you, too," Juni admits, patting my head affectionately. "Once Ari is gone, we will have no heir to the Unicorn's blessing, and all the realms will be in danger of falling apart."

She looks out the window of my room, and I follow her gaze. The sky is full of rainbows as the evening draws near.

THE REALMS BEYOND THE RAINBOW

Juni is right, but she is also wrong. The king has already been facing opposition, as there are growing factions within the kingdom that oppose his rule. If they were to find out that the Unicorn's blessing is no longer on the Queen's household, it will be the end of Toulacoeur.

And the end of my life, too.

After Cari was kidnapped, Kleon vowed only to come back when she returned. The queen has suffered in sickness since then, both at the loss of her daughter and the rejection of her unicorn protector.

Princess Cari is now the only one who is able to summon Kleon to the kingdom, and since I am not really her, no matter how much I may look like her, I will be branded a traitor to the people of the Honeyspice Lands and their leader, the Alpha Kitsune.

It is my duty, as a slave to the king and queen, not to let the kingdom know the truth about Cari's fate; they might eventually find out the truth, but the sooner they do, the sooner I die, executed as a traitor.

Trying not to think of my worst possible fate, I follow Juni out of my room down to join the procession.

The sun has fully set now, and the rainbows of the skies are now bathed in moonlight.

Kiro is standing behind his parents, holding the reins of two horses. One is for me, and the other is

THE REALMS BEYOND THE RAINBOW

for him. I will be riding next to him as we visit the capital, before we return to the courtyard gardens for Kiro's birthday ball.

I straighten as I walk gallantly down to meet them. I know I am not truly worthy of their love and affection, but I want to be.

CHAPTER TWO

The castle of Toulacoeur is as grand as its heritage, with its sturdy walls, painted roofs, and marble floors. There are five sides, with a tower at each point, providing a line of both defense and rest to its inhabitants. The towers are joined together with walls and love along with the sandstone and marble, or so the legend goes, and, much like the tiara on my head, the tallest tower stands firm and proud in the middle of the castle. It's so tall, it seems to pierce the sky.

Inside, the castle is adorned with different relics and trimmings from the seven realms. All of it shines with polish and cleaning, especially on days like today, and no one but the most astute observer can see where the decorative carvings are being eaten out by woodmites and how the gilded arches are in need of repairs from the last season's rain damage.

I think of this as I sit in my royal chair, at the high end of the garden's temporary dance floor, close to where rows of tables have been set up for dinner.

Having toured the main roads around Auralis on horseback, we came back to the courtyard gardens just inside the keep. Kiro's party was ready; the orchestra was playing, the decorations were perfectly arranged, and the feast was prepared. All we had to do was offer prayer, and then the celebration officially commenced. Since then, I've sat through several rounds of dancing and eating, watching it all happen.

It is as if I am more of a ghostly spectator than a full flesh and blood participant. I am sure many of the people are interested in seeing me, but the king and queen are very protective. They say it is because of the time when "I" was five, back when I managed to get free from the castle guard long enough for a stranger to pick me up and take me away, mistaking me for a poor child.

That is the official story, not the real one.

The real story is that Princess Cari took ill, and one of her attendants, after it was shown that she would live, stole her out of the castle under the cover of night. Queen Arianna and Kiro, who had been only three years old at the time, were also sick with a fever, so no one noticed the lost princess in time to stop her kidnapper.

After the initial discovery and upheaval, and then my introduction as the "found princess," the king and queen quietly searched throughout the lands for her, to no avail.

They still send out search parties under false pretenses from time to time, in hopes of finding their missing daughter.

Juni told me and Kiro once, when we kept peppering her with questions, that the queen summoned Kleon after Cari was taken, and he'd told her that the princess was no longer in any realm inside Toulacoeur. Then Kleon told the queen he would not return until Cari called for him.

I have never understood that. Kleon is the guardian of Toulacoeur, and the christened ambassador for God.

From what I'd heard, I knew God was supposed to be a god of compassion and righteousness. Queen Arianna had been the Unicorn Keeper for nearly three decades, and she had been, from what I knew, a generous ruler who was happy with her family and served her nation with pride. I still don't understand why Kleon would leave her, especially when it was clear she needed him. Her heart must have shattered when Cari disappeared.

Kiro says I am right: the queen's heart shattered, right along with her nerves. Since Cari's disappearance, Queen Arianna often spends long days in bed and has trouble with anxiety, especially when I am around her. I don't think she likes the reminder, even if the kingdom needs the illusion I offer.

I turn to watch her now, sitting just a few seats down from me. Her hand is shaking as she holds a cup up to her lips. If I squint, I can see the silver streaks lighting up her own dull, golden hair, despite her hairdressers' best efforts to cover or hide them.

My disguise as Princess Cari is based on the paintings of both the queen and the princess

THE REALMS BEYOND THE RAINBOW

throughout their lives. Every year—or at least, every year before the kidnapping—each royal had a portrait done. After Cari disappeared, the queen decided it was "too risky" for the people to see the royal family members. The last official portrait of the princess at five years old still hangs in the gathering hall of the castle, though since my arrival, the eyes have been changed.

The queen has changed much since her last portrait, too. Her hair and lips are much thinner; her body is barely more than skin and bone. I have to squeeze my natural build into Cari's chosen form to make it look like being lithe is part of the heritage, thanks to the queen's ongoing deterioration.

"Your Highness, Princess Cari the Luminous."

Inwardly, I groan as I am approached by several ambassadors from the different realms. Ever since Princess Cari turned sixteen—since I was fourteen—many have come seeking her hand in marriage. Celebrations like this have allowed for me to hear more proposals.

Even just a few generations ago, the king and queens of Toulacoeur would have lots of children and marry them to different parts of Toulacoeur's seven realms. But Queen Arianna is an only child, and she was not able to have children after Kiro was born.

I don't know what I will do if the king and queen force me into a marriage; it is not as though Princess Cari is actually here to marry anyone. As much as I

THE REALMS BEYOND THE RAINBOW

have always tried to do my duty, it would not be possible for me to conceal my true nature from a spouse indefinitely.

Thankfully, Queen Arianna has let it be known that she needs me beside her while she faces her degenerative health. It is definitely a lie; I know she wants to believe that Kleon and Cari will both come back to her yet.

But it is a kind lie, one that protects me from a marital alliance for now.

I do my best to keep this kindness in mind as I smile and make nice with those who offer.

The Clan of the Redstone Dragon steps forward first, all five of their ambassadors moving in perfect, synchronized steps. They are *always* the ones who offer first, and they always do it with such austerity. I clench my hands in my lap.

I acknowledge them, and the second they are able to stand up straight, they do. The Clan does not like to bow to anyone, even if they are under our rule. Redstone heritage runs thick in King Dario's blood, especially in their aristocracy. As they stand before me, I notice they share the same tough jawline as the king. They have their alabaster hair swept back from their foreheads, and their long, crimson robes make me think of blood.

Their leader steps forward, and I recognize him. It was the leader of the high guard, Dayyon Erdawan, of the House of Midor. His eyes are like slits, with their rust-colored irises sunken into his skin under thick, charcoal eyebrows. As a Dayyon, he held one of the highest ranks among the Redstone clan, and he seemed well suited to handling authority. I silently groan to myself; I did not enjoy meeting him last year, and it is not hard for me to believe I will not like our encounter this year.

"We have come here to request the honor of your hand in marriage to the Redstone Clanmaster's eldest son."

"I humbly thank you for your generous offer, Honorable Dayyon Erdawan," I say, trying to sound as confident in my supposed power as Princess Cari would have been. "But as my lady mother lives and breathes, I will not accept a proposal that would take me far away from her side."

Erdawan's smile is as false as my own disguise, but as I finish answering him, it only grows into a more pleased, almost sinister grin.

"The Clanmaster knows this, and he has great respect for your familial piety," Erdawan agrees. His voice is like velvet, and I grow more nervous the more he speaks. "This is the precise reason he wishes to engage you to his son. I regret to say the Clanmaster himself is facing the last years of his life. He has sent me to inform his cousin, your father the king, that he would like to see his son married before his passing."

I gulp. Never had any realm dared to question my response when I said no to their proposal. The king and queen's position on my marriage was well-known, and I could only remind Erdawan of that as I sat there.

"I am very sorry to hear of the Clanmaster's health," I reply, glancing around the ambassador's faces again. The Redstone Clan is known for their seriousness, but I could see traces of their hidden sadness. My heart grieves for them; they are not alone in wondering about the future of their realm and working to make it as bright as possible.

"It would be for the best for our Clan to solidify our lineage," Erdawan continues. "I'm sure as you know from your own position, weakness is not long tolerated before insurgency rises in its place."

"The king, uh, my father, is indeed sympathetic to your realm's plight," I reply. My voice is softer now, but remains firm. "We will consider your offer with the utmost consideration."

I glance around Erdawan, looking at the other nations who have come to the party to see me. While I am relieved to see there are fewer than there were last year, there are still plenty of other marriage proposals I will have to endure before the night is gone.

There are messengers from the Shadowcavern Dwarves, dressed in their amethyst-trimmed armor, waiting in solid, sturdy patience; there is tension further down the line, as the Gryphon Riders from the Dovelion Warlords are glaring harshly at the Turqs, the sea nomads from the outer shores of Toulacoeur. There have been rumors lately that their realms' peace treaty and the resulting marriage has not been going well. I have to smother a laugh at some of the wild reports of the Turq's nymphaean bride and her very public battles against the Warlord's youngest princeling.

Thankfully, no one has come from the Honeyspice Lands. The thought of another kitsunefolk makes me shiver. I did not grow up around my kind, but from what I know about them, they would be able to recognize me if I am not extremely careful. Kitsunefolk, all of them, no matter their class, are very sensitive to other changelings.

I breathe a little easier, but that is before Erdawan takes another step forward. He is clearly unhappy my attention has shifted away from him.

"The people of Redstone have been your family's devoted servants for many years, ever since our blood has been linked through marriage and offspring. If anyone can understand your family's needs, it is ours." Erdawan steps forward and pulls something small out from his pocket.

When he holds it toward me, I gasp, and then cough, caught by surprise.

In his hand is a red diamond—one much larger than the one that was supposed to be in my Unicorn tiara.

"As you know, Princess Cari, red diamonds are extremely rare," Erdawan says. His eyes flicker over my crown, where the red ruby rests at its center. "We have carried this precious gem throughout the other realms in order to present it to you as an engagement present. It might be for the best for the king and queen to agree in this matter, considering their own history of failing to keep such treasures—including your own—safe."

Does he know about Princess Cari?

I remain still as I stare at him, paralyzed by the possibility.

Erdawan studies me. "There wouldn't be any other extenuating circumstances as to why you would deny my Clan's offer of marriage, would there?"

I can feel the tremble of my lips as I press them together. The small pressure helps me focus, and I am careful not to let my changeling skills falter as I watch him. I don't want to say anything that will get me in trouble with the king and queen, but Erdawan leaves me very little choice.

Erdawan's expression grows more insidious at each passing second.

Does he think he's gotten the better of me?

"What do you think, Princess Cari?" Erdawan asks. "No matter the jewels we offer, it is still our trust that is the greatest asset between our nations."

Despite how sinister he looks, Erdawan is right about that.

"That is true," I say with a gallant nod. "And I am grateful for your consideration. If it is trust that you value most, then I only ask for the same in return. You must trust me when I say the king and the queen will decide my fate."

Erdawan's eyes widen ever so slightly in surprise, and I know I've caught him off guard.

I nearly laugh at the sight; I've lived my whole life surrounded by kingdom politics. The last thing he wants is to be asked to give of himself what he is asking of me.

At his silence, I wave him away as gently as possible. "As you can see, Dayyon, I have other guests to attend to. Please feel free to put in a request to see my father and mother before you go. I know there is a line to see them, but there is plenty of time tonight; the festivities will be going long into the morning hours for Kiro's birthday celebration."

"Wait." Erdawan holds up his hand. The other ambassadors behind him stall in their departure. "I have a question for you, Princess."

I sigh under my breath. "What is it?"

"You will not object to the fate assigned to you by the king and queen?"

I hate how he talks; it is as if he knows I am a fraud, that he knows my life cannot end well, with the real Princess Cari nowhere to be found and the realms starting to show signs of hostility towards one another.

"Of course I will." My chin lifts, in a manner I hope looks as defiant as much as it does delicate, and I straighten in my small throne. "It would take Kleon the Unicorn himself to alter my fate."

"It is interesting that you should bring him up," Erdawan says. "Perhaps you should call him, and see what he says in this matter? Your family is so close to him, after all."

I frown at him now. "It is not wise to question my fealty to the kingdom in this way, especially if it is possible I will one day be part of your clan. I would hate to be in a position where I would have to question your loyalty, too."

"Such a spirited princess you are." His lips are tight, and his jaw is clenched as he speaks.

"That is why the Clanmaster's son seeks my hand, I am sure," I say, starting to enjoy our political sparring. "Unless he prefers for everyone around him to be in dull agreement with him?"

Erdawan's forehead crinkles in exasperation. "I suppose after all those stories of how you've been seen at different balls sporting a foxtail and cat ears, it is only natural you should tempt fate so often."

"I am afraid tempting fate is a family trait, Dayyon." Kiro's voice cuts through the crowd before he appears. He brushes past Erdawan easily, giving the man a curt but respectful nod. He stands before me and reaches out his hand. "And I do believe it is my turn."

I can hear Erdawan as he shifts behind Kiro. "Princess Cari and I are in the middle of a discussion of the future, Prince Kiro."

"We can talk about the future in the future," Kiro replies. "For the present, I'd like to take my lovely sister out on the dance floor. It wouldn't be proper if I favored one realm above the other, would it?"

Despite the frustration I see from the Redstone Clan, and the disappointment from the other realm's ambassadors, I take Kiro's hand, and together, we head for the garden's brightly lit dance floor.

CHAPTER THREE

❖   ❖   ❖   ❖

The moment Erdawan is out of earshot, I let out of a sigh of relief. "Thank you, Kiro."

"Anything for you, Kitty," Kiro whispers back. "Besides, I didn't like how he was looking at you."

"He is very determined to get Cari to marry into their clan. We should tell the king and queen." I shiver, recalling the fear I'd felt in front of Erdawan.

"They already know." Kiro shifts his hands as he takes me into his arms, and we begin to dance. "They shouldn't have let the Dayyon talk to you. He is very ruthless, even among the Redstone Clan."

I snort playfully. "I've noticed."

"The queen has mentioned he has a reputation for being less than honorable," Kiro says.

"At least he is forced to present himself as honorable while he is here."

"True." Kiro glances back to look at the Dayyon, who is watching both of us with an irritated gaze. Kiro waves at him playfully, and we laugh when Erdawan's eyes only darken.

I stop a moment later, remembering Erdawan's remarks about duty and trust. "I should be more careful," I whisper. "I think he suspects something is wrong with me."

"There is nothing wrong with you," Kiro assures me, drawing me closer to him. I am very aware of his body, as we move together to the music, and while he is leading me properly around the ballroom, the way a brother should lead his sister around the dancefloor, there is no brotherly affection in his burning eyes.

I almost trip on my skirt as we make another turn, and Kiro clears his throat.

"Kitty." He whispers my name softly, so softly I almost don't hear him over the music. "There is something I need to talk to you about."

Remembering our earlier time together in my room, I feel the heat rise in my cheeks. Instantly, I feel the mask of my changeling talents slip. I don't have to look in a mirror to know the fox-like marks under my eyes have blossomed into sight, outlined by the black lines that mark me as one of the kitsunefolk.

"Maybe it would be best to wait." Ducking my head, I rush to correct my mistake. I desperately hope the Dayyon—and all the other realm ambassadors— are not able to see me.

"I don't think that's a good idea," Kiro says. He hasn't noticed the seconds where it was my face looking up at him, rather than Cari's; he is looking over at the ambassadors, and I wonder if he'd sensed my distress. "I should've said something earlier, but … I just couldn't."

THE REALMS BEYOND THE RAINBOW

I pull back from him as I feel my transformation waver again.

What is going on? Why am I having such trouble keeping my disguise?

It is a struggle to keep Cari's features in place, and with each second that passes, my fear increases. If I don't get myself under control, I risk disgracing the kingdom, making a scene, and possibly committing treason against the king and queen. And at Kiro's birthday celebration, no less.

"Kitty?"

My heart lurches as I realize the truth.

It's Kiro.

"Kiro," I breath out his name in terror, as I realize my love for him is compromising me. My ears begin to slide out from underneath the golden crown of hair.

He tries to steady me in his arms, but I push him away. "Excuse me," I say, my voice frantic. "I have to go."

"Wait, don't—"

As I cover my face with my hands and weave my way through the crowds surrounding the dancefloor, I can hear Kiro trying to follow me.

I find refuge in a small cluster of trees. I can still hear Kiro calling for "Cari" to come back, but I know it's too risky yet. I need at least a moment, perhaps two.

I can't help but grimace as I take care to reassert my disguise. I'd been so worried about Erdawan's ruthlessness revealing my true self, it had never crossed my mind that my love for Kiro could betray me.

A laugh escapes me. After he'd almost kissed me earlier, and now, after I almost exposed my kitsune heritage, I know now I will have to tell Kiro the truth.

I have to tell Kiro I am in love with him, and because of that, it is harder for me to maintain my changeling farce.

As I stand there in the trees, shielded by the shadows, my heart strangely fills with hope and daring. It is true I don't know what my fate will be, or how much longer I will be able to serve the king and queen as their pretend daughter. But I am grateful for my time in their care, and I can forgive the worst moments of palace life—and there were plenty—all because of the goodness Kiro brought me.

Resolved and reestablished as Princess Cari, I step out into the light once more.

Horns blare into the night, and the dancing music dies. Everyone, including me, turns to the front table, where King Dario begins to speak.

"To all the realms of Toulacoeur, we welcome you to Auralis, the capital of our beloved home."

As he stands next to the queen, I can see King Dario is dressed in his finest robes, with minimal armor. He is still a tall figure of strength, but in recent years, that strength has dimmed as his hair has thinned. There are several years between him and Queen Arianna, but with her nervousness and her melancholy spells, she seems even older than he is.

I know the king to be a harder man, but Juni's devotion to him and the queen over the years has softened that image. They were both egregiously shaken at Cari's loss, and further at the uncertainty of her fate.

Cari had been the light of their lives, and now that she's gone, they live in perpetual shadows. Not even Kiro, for all that I love him, can fully brighten their lives. I have failed in this area, too, and, thanks to all my lapses in my disguise or in my mannerisms, I probably add to their pain.

Realizing that Kiro is standing on the other side of his mother, I groan. I am supposed to be up there for the introductions and toasts.

So much for not disappointing them further.

As King Dario stands before the crowds now, introducing the higher-ranking members of the realms and their children, I carefully and quietly make my way toward the front, hoping no one will notice my absence too much. Thankfully, the king has a commanding voice. Everyone is listening to him as I make my way to the front of the dancefloor.

THE REALMS BEYOND THE RAINBOW

Everyone except me.

Which is why, just as I straighten the Unicorn tiara on my head, when he says Kiro's name, it is as though a fog lifts inside of me.

"—ask all of you to raise your glasses to my son, Prince Kiro, and his soon-to-be-wife, Lady Ariella, of the Gryphon Riders from the Dovelion Warlords."

Cheers and clapping erupts throughout the castle grounds, as I feel the earth drop from under my feet.

"No." No one hears my whisper of discord. Tears fill my eyes as though I'd been slapped across my face.

My steps come to a stop as I watch Kiro extend his hand to a beautiful lady, one who is wrapped up in an extravagant gown of golden silk. Even from where I am, I see her eyes are a sparkling amber, and her face is pleasant and radiant as she looks on Kiro.

How could she not be happy? Kiro is a true prize among princes.

And how could he not be pleased with her, either?

Lady Ariella is clearly very beautiful, and the daughter of a Gryphon Rider. The Dovelion Warlord leads one of the wealthiest tribes, always experimenting with new weaponry.

When I remember this, it makes more sense to me. The Warlords have been known to cause trouble for King Dario from time to time; with their production lines and their skilled craftmanship, the

Warlords are always developing new weapons and working their way into one-sided alliances.

Perhaps this is even one of them.

But as I watch Kiro and Ariella stand before the crowds, the last of any hope I had in my heart collapses in on itself and dies. I am unable to move, either back to the woods for cover or up to the front with the rest of my household.

King Dario is clearly pleased by the reactions of the masses. "My family is very thankful for your company tonight, as we celebrate the announcement of—"

It is just at that moment when a loud *boom* echoes throughout the sky, and a streak of fire crosses overhead.

A shooting star?

My eyes are wide as I see the strange meteor. I've never seen anything like it; it burns blue and orange, passing through the lunar rainbows, the moonlight reflecting off patches of white, with the occasional red stripes and blue stars.

The crowd, torn between being mesmerized and terrified, begin questioning what is is and where it came from, and what it is doing here.

Their questions and chatter are muffled as I put my hands over my ears; the deafening blast of its impact, even from this distance, sends out a strong ripple of wind and earth.

THE REALMS BEYOND THE RAINBOW

As the dust blows past and the earth settles, no one is talking anymore.

And that is when I hear her.

"No!" Queen Arianna has fallen to her knees. "No, this is a sign! It cannot be anything else."

The whispers stir up again, though this time the crowds are more certain of what is happening.

The queen is having an anxiety spell. She is screaming and crying, and at her sadness, I hurry forward.

I cannot look at Kiro—cannot look at him, think of him, cannot do anything with him—while the queen suffers.

I step out of the crowd just as Juni takes over her care.

"Majesty, it's all right," she whispers softly, patting Queen Arianna's brow with a handkerchief. "Come now, let's go to the palace. We can take you to your room."

"Mother." Kiro is there, too, and I have to scoot to the other side of Juni.

"It's a sign," the queen murmurs. "Danger is coming, the end of the kingdom. It's here. It has to be here, Juni."

"Your Majesty?" I approach her quietly, ignoring Kiro as he hesitates. "It's me. Princess Cari."

"Cari! Cari, no!"

Juni and a few of the other handmaidens help pick up the queen, keeping her balanced as they lead her away.

Behind me, the king has tried to take command of the audience, reciting the opening lines of his toast to Kiro and Ariella. He calms down the people, assuring them that it was but a shooting star while I help the queen and her servants head back to the palace.

The music starts up, and Kiro and Ariella are to take the floor in celebration of their engagement.

At that, I hurry even more to keep pace with Juni and the others.

But when Juni sees me, she pulls me aside.

"Keep the queen comfortable and settle her into her rooms," Juni orders the others as they continue forward. "I will alert the bathmaster she will need an herbal bath."

"Kleon, Kleon, where are you? Why are you doing this to me?"

Juni and I both wince at the queen's cries, and from the look on Juni's face, I know she is more concerned than she will admit.

"Ari's had a worse time of things lately," Juni whispers. "It's close to the anniversary of Cari's disappearance."

"Do you think she's right about the shooting star?" I ask.

"Pish, don't be so superstitious, Honeyspice," Juni barks. "Remember, God is bigger than us, and he's bigger than Ari's troubles, too."

"But God has been known to send signs in the skies before," I remind her.

"We'll worry about it later. Right now Ari needs her care," Juni says, nodding back toward the shaking queen.

I watch as she enters the castle with all her attendants. She is so frail and helpless, and I hope the king managed to distract everyone from seeing her as such.

"Perhaps it is better if you stay away from her for a little while. I will see to her." Juni pats my shoulder and then ruffles my hair. She frets over me as much as she still does to the queen, and her gentleness is a gift in that moment. "You could use a break from playing Princess Cari, too."

"What do you mean by that?" I ask.

"Oh, Honeyspice." Juni embraces me briefly. "You'll need to fix yourself before you go into the castle. But take a few moments for yourself. I know this has been a hard night for you."

She briefly cups my cheek and then leaves me there, alone.

CHAPTER FOUR

❖   ❖   ❖   ❖

I don't know how many moments pass before I realize I am cold. The queen is inside the castle, and the others with her are too. I am alone.

I am cold and alone, outside the grand castle of Auralis, the capital of Toulacoeur, the home of power for all the realms. Nothing about this power comforts me, and everything about it angers me, saddens me—maybe even destroys me.

Perhaps it has destroyed Queen Arianna already.

Who can save me from my fate now?

I have no answer to that as I fold my hands together in unconscious prayer.

It is possible that the God of Toulacoeur could still save me, isn't it?

I am a slave here in this place of power, but I have heard he was able to set the captive free, that he sent Kleon to us in order to watch over us. I've heard he was a god of love, caring for us as a father cared for his beloved children.

I don't know much about that. The king is my master, not my father, and even though my life is maintained only because of his graciousness, I don't feel like I am truly part of his family.

I bow my head, close my eyes, and whisper, "If you are able to hear me, Father God, I would like to be free of this place." My prayer is a desperate prayer, one spoken out of hopelessness and humbled heartbreak.

I open my eyes, hoping to see the world before me change, but there is nothing there to suggest my prayer has been heard, much less answered.

Orphaned, enslaved, and now abandoned.

I've never had a real family, and the only boy I've ever loved is marrying someone else.

There is either no god, or he is not as compassionate as I believed.

I let out a sigh that stems from the deepest, loneliest part of my soul. My head falls into my hands, and it feels as though I have nothing else left.

There is a stirring sound in the wind behind me.

"Are we going on our adventure early tonight?"

Kiro's voice, once soothing, now stings.

I flinch as he approaches me, hurrying to wipe away my tears and remake Cari's face. Her face is the best mask between us, and the reminder of my duty gives me the courage.

"I doubt it," I reply, pursing my lips as I hear my voice croaking. I swallow my unshed tears and force the lump in my throat to leave. "The queen is very distraught over the shooting star."

"She is distraught over most things, and this should not surprise you," Kiro says.

His voice is firm, something I did not expect from him.

"You'll have to excuse my concern," I say. "It's not like we would expect a shooting star at all, either."

"The king will send his guards to investigate the star. There is no point in worrying about it, until we know what it is, or if it's anything unusual at all. But I don't want to talk about that anymore," he says. "I want to talk about earlier."

"Oh, yes," I say, stepping away from him. "Congratulations on your engagement. I should have given you my support before I'd left the crowd. The king wasn't upset over my behavior, was he? I'd hate to think I'd ruined your night."

"Kitty—"

"And then the queen was so upset, too," I say, retreating another step. "I'm sure I can just let them know I was too tired to think clearly, and that is the truth, really. I'm tired, and I want to go to bed after I make sure the queen is doing well."

"Kitty."

My back comes up against a tree trunk, and I almost fall as my feet stumble over its roots. Kiro grabs my shoulders and steadies me.

"Enough," he whispers. "I know you're upset about Ariella."

I hate how he says her name, without any trace of disgust.

"Just because I didn't wish you all the happiness in the world out there doesn't mean I don't want it for you," I snap, my voice breaking this time as I felt my façade collapse again.

Kiro holds onto me even more tightly. "I was only told about it earlier today." Kiro leans down, forcing me to look at him. "I wanted to tell you, but—"

"Please, just leave me alone." I don't really want to hear what he has to say. All I want to do is leave him before I start to cry. My hands push against him, but he doesn't budge.

"I don't love her, Kitty. You know that, don't you? I love *you*."

And then before I can blink or breathe or even think, I am crying, and he is kissing me, and I am kissing him back.

Despite the saltiness of my tears, I've never tasted anything sweeter. I stop pushing him away, and I cling to him. My fingers dig into his hair and he leans into me as he lifts me up in his arms.

"Kitty." His lips whisper my name as he goes to kiss me again. My knees buckle, and I fear I will fall over at the joy and warmth I feel inside.

THE REALMS BEYOND THE RAINBOW

Kiro pulls back from me, long enough to brush the tears away from my face, although they are happy ones now.

"There you are." He smiles. "I always love seeing your real face."

"Kiro." I want to tell him everything. I want to tell him that he brings my true self out despite any disguise; that even though I don't know the day or hour I fell in love with him, I know I don't ever want there to be a moment where I don't love him ever again.

But already he is leaning down and kissing me again, and I am already responding to him. His hands tangle into my hair, and Princess Cari's Unicorn tiara falls to the ground as my ears perk open.

I hear a gasp of shock and disbelief behind us.

"Kiro!"

I don't have to look over to know it is the king.

Kiro turns to face his father, but won't let me run away. As the king looks at me, I silently scream in terror.

This is it. This is the end.

I realize this all over again as I see who is walking with him. It is Ariella's father, one of the Gryphon Riders, the man who had been just moments before toasting to Kiro's engagement to his daughter.

THE REALMS BEYOND THE RAINBOW

I stop fighting Kiro's hold. There is nothing I can do to save myself now; I must submit to my fate, as I always knew I would.

Kiro stands his ground. "Father, I—"

"I don't want to hear it, Kiro." King Dario's voice is grating. He signals behind him, calling for his guards.

"No," Kiro objects. He finally lets me go as he moves to talk with the king. "You can't do this."

I can't seem to find my voice, to tell him that it is no use; I know watching Kiro be brave and fight for me will be the last time I am allowed to see him.

"I can't do this?" The king's voice is as sharp as a knife, cutting through the air. "*You* can't do this. We have an agreement with Warlord Gonzo, and you will honor it."

Kiro remains unmoved. "I love Kitty. I don't want to marry someone I don't love."

"Your marriage to Lady Ariella will ensure peace." The king scoffs. "What good will 'Kitty' do for you, when the realms rise up against us and then each other?"

Warlord Gonzo, Ariella's father, steps forward, a frown on his face as he studies me. "I hope you are not considering going back on your word, King Dario. Toulacoeur is already facing enough issues. I thought you wanted an alliance with my guild."

"We do, Gonzo, my friend," the king assures him. "You'll have to excuse my son's poor behavior. He must be under a fox fire spell from the kitsune girl. They are known for their trickster ways."

The guards take hold of me before I can remind the king that I am not able to conjure up fox fire, that I was only born with my changeling talent.

I suppose it does not matter, either way; I will still be punished.

"Kitty." Kiro steps in front of me. "No, Father. You can't hurt her."

"Kiro, please." The king softens his voice, sounding more sympathetic. "You're not in your right mind, son. This girl has obviously tricked you!"

The king looks down at me and lets out a horrific gasp. "She has even stolen Princess Cari's outfit and crown!"

"You didn't lose your daughter again, did you?" Gonzo's smug look makes even me want to fight him. "And to a Kitsunefolk, no less?"

"Where is my daughter?" King Dario takes Gonzo's taunting as a signal to advance on me. My ears shake with fear, and I bite down on my lips to stop myself from screaming.

Kiro protects me, standing between me and the king. "I know what happened to Cari. I would hate to reveal all the details to you, Father, if I feel so threatened."

Kiro's veiled threat is clear. "Kiro, please stop," I whisper.

Kiro is a good son; seeing him threaten to reveal the truth about Cari's unresolved disappearance is scandalous.

Does he love me this much? Truly?

Does he love me enough to stand up to his father, risk his marriage with the kingdom's ally, and reveal his nation's darkest, deepest, most carefully guarded secret?

Kiro looks at me again, as if I'd asked my questions aloud, and I know I have to stop him. He will only bring ruin upon himself at this rate.

I can die happy just knowing he loves me. And I am likely going to die anyway.

"Kiro," I whisper, trying to warn him. "You're only going to get in trouble if you keep this up."

Kiro shakes his head. "Kitty, I'm not going to—"

The king hisses another warning to Kiro, threatening Kiro with everything he has—whispering how he would even use my comfort and safety as bargaining chips, if it comes down to that.

I don't fight against the guards as they lead me away; I know my place.

I can never be with Kiro.

"No," Kiro yells. "No, don't do this."

"Take him to his room," King Dario says, waving his arm. "He'll need some time for that magic spell to wear off."

"I'm not under a spell," Kiro insists as he fights to get back to me. The guards grab onto him and hold him back fiercely.

It is too late.

It is too late for him, it is too late for me, and it is too late for us.

"Kiro, stop fighting," I cry, unable to watch as one of the guards elbows him in the side. He emits a painful grunt, but I am forced into the castle before I can hear him say anything other than my name in response.

Once we are out of the king's sight, the guards march onward to the dungeon. I don't intentionally mean to drag my feet as I walk, but I can't seem to force myself to move properly. Princess Cari's dress is muddled with grass stains and some dirt, the only evidence I have of my stolen moments of happiness.

When we arrive, a cell is ready for me, one with a small window at the top and iron slabs to hold me inside. It is dirty and smelly, and there is only a small bed, one that looks hard and cold. I involuntarily shiver at the sight of it.

Still, I am grateful when I am only thrown into the cell, and not chained down. I am able to walk and pace within the small prison; I can also look up through the small window, seeking out the moonlight.

My tears are gone now. My hands are steady. I don't know what will happen to me.

I don't know what will happen to Kiro.

All I do know is that I am stuck in this place for the moment, but I am loved. That is enough to grant me peace while I wait.

As the dawn peeks out over the horizon, I think of my earlier prayer, how I had prayed to be free of the palace. Instead of being free of this place, I'd only been sent further into it as a permanent prison.

THE REALMS BEYOND THE RAINBOW

CHAPTER FIVE

A loud clanging noise rings out from outside the dungeon, and I jump awake at the noise.

I don't know how much time has passed since the night before: the light is dull from outside my barred window. My natural senses are no help; my body is stiff, my stomach is growling, and my head aches the most.

I press my hands to my temples, digging into them as the commotion from outside reiterates itself, this time accompanied by different people shouting and yelling at each other.

Of all the voices I hear, I recognize two for sure: Queen Arianna's and Kiro's.

Something is wrong.

Is someone coming to sentence me already?

I swallow hard, noticing the taste of bile in my mouth.

Hardly a morning passes when I wake up and feel like a princess, even though I have been playing one, but today, I feel every inch the status of my slavehood, even as I remain in Princess Cari's once-lovely evening gown.

The door to the dungeon opens with a snap, and I gasp as I see Kiro struggling with a pair of guards as they drag him toward a cell of his own.

"That will be all, guardsmen." The queen's voice is sharp and distinctive against the dungeon.

"You can't do this to me!" Kiro fights back, but they throw him in and lock the door.

"Actually, I can," the queen responds. "Your behavior has been appalling, Kiro!"

"Kiro." I inch closer to him, but he holds up a hand in my direction.

He is telling me to wait, and I obligingly scoot back as Kiro continues to argue with his mother.

"How can you do this to us, Kiro?" Queen Arianna waves her hand in my direction, and I suspect that out of the two of us, I had a better night's sleep. Her hair is wild, and her eyes are wide. Her gown is wrinkled, and she has no shoes on. Her voice is more than weary as she begins to cry. "The kingdom is falling apart, and you would burn the rest of it to the ground, and all for a slave girl?"

"She wouldn't be a slave if you hadn't made her one," Kiro argues.

"Excellent idea," Queen Arianna snaps back. Her tears are gone, and her face is angry now. "We'll execute her then, as we could have done when she was first brought here."

"You do, and I'll tell everyone the real reason Kleon left." Kiro juts his chin forward in defiance. "Not to mention, you'll lose Cari again, until you can find another replacement—if I don't tell everyone that she's gone, too."

"You wouldn't dare."

They argue over the kingdom and its future, their voices so full of pain and passion I barely notice as Juni comes into the dungeon's doorway. She carefully steps up to comfort Queen Arianna.

"Majesty, please." Juni soothes her hair back from her face, much the same as she'd done to me before Kiro's ball. "You need time to recover."

"It's that shooting star's fault. No, wait … this is all Kleon's fault," the queen hisses. "No. No, this is all *her* fault!"

I am surprised when she turns around and points to me.

"How is this my fault?" I ask, unable to stop myself from asking, even though I am risking her retribution.

Before she can answer me, Juni manages to get the queen to settle down. Juni leads her out of the dungeon, and Arianna only turns back when she reaches the door.

"You can stay here until we've decided what to do with you," the queen says, looking at both Kiro and me. All of her rage and hatred is fully displayed on her haggard face. "If the two of you will not do as you're told, I will find a way to make you. By Kleon, I swear I will."

The dungeon slams shut, and I feel a little sympathy for the queen. It was true Kleon stopped coming to see her when Cari was lost. As her footsteps trail off into the distance, I wonder if she is so desperate to see him again that she doesn't even realize how lost she is.

I stare after her, barely noticing as Kiro pulls something out of his belt. At the sound of metal clicking on metal, I turn to see that he is picking the lock on his cell with a long, twisted wire.

"Kiro." His name comes out of my lips as more of a whimper than a whisper, but he doesn't seem to hear me.

Once he is free, he comes over to me and begins to pick the lock on my cell. "Sorry it took so long for me to get here," he says.

"Why are you here, Kiro?" His hair falls over his eyes in a charming way as he works, and I want so much to reach through the bars and fix it for him.

"I'm here for you, of course. My father is preoccupied with that shooting star investigation, and Mother, of course, is upset."

"I noticed," I say apologetically. "I hope you didn't make it worse for her."

"I couldn't make it look like I was going easy on them, now could I?" As he speaks, the lock clicks and falls away. Kiro opens my cell and comes for me. He peels me off the floor and embraces me.

I love him, but I still hesitate. "What will happen to you when they find out we're free?"

"I'm more concerned with what will happen to me if you stay here." Kiro sets his jaw. "My parents might see you as a slave, but you've always been more to me."

"And you've always been more to me," I whisper back. "But I don't want you to get hurt."

"Then run away with me."

I hear him say the words, but I don't understand him. "Run away?"

"Yes. We can go live in one of the other realms."

"What about your parents' treaty with the Gryphon Riders?" I bite my lip. "What about Ariella?"

"I already told you, I love you, Kitty." He wraps his arms around me. "Not her. I barely even know her. There's no love lost between us, I'm sure."

"But what about peace? Would you really sacrifice the entire future of the kingdom for me, Kiro?"

"Yes." There is no hesitation in his eyes, and for the first time, I am horrified.

THE REALMS BEYOND THE RAINBOW

"What? How could you say that? These are your people. All of Toulacoeur's realms depend on you to keep the peace." I back away from him. "My life is nothing, Kiro. Nothing compared to all of theirs."

"Your life is important, too," Kiro insists. He takes my hand and pulls me, even as I dig in my heels and try to slow him down as we reach the dungeon entrance. "Come with me."

"No, Kiro. Please stop," I yell in protest.

It is likely at my volume that Kiro finally stops. He puts a finger on my lips, and I obey him out of lifelong habit more than anything else. I can't let him do this; I can't let him give up everything for me.

What would we do? Where would we go? And what about all the others?

"We can't do this," I whisper, sliding out of his grip.

I've grown up surrounded by all the king and queen's finest resources. I've seen their guards and the soldiers that fight for them. I know there is no hope of escape.

And I think I can be fine with that.

I am fine with giving up, with playing my role. I have Kiro's love, and that is enough—that is even too much! The idea that he would love me, that he would want me, that he would do as much as he is apparently set on doing, all to have me is wonderfully asinine, and as much as I love him for loving me, I don't want him to risk anything for me. And that includes the lives of other people throughout the seven realms.

"Kitty." Kiro runs his hands through his hair again. I can tell he is vacillating, weighing his options, and that there is something he doesn't want to tell me but I've now forced his hand. "Don't worry about the kingdom. It doesn't matter anymore."

"Of course it does!" I feel the blood drain from my face as I recall how furious the king was at my deceit. "You can't exchange everyone else's life for mine."

"My parents already have!" Kiro sighs and shakes his head.

At this, I stop moving. There is a chill in the stillness of the air all around me. Queen Arianna's words echo in my mind. Is it my fault after all, that we are in this position?

"What do you mean?" I ask.

"Do you know why Kleon denounced my mother after Cari was kidnapped?"

"I thought it was because Cari disappeared that he stopped coming when the queen summoned him."

"No." Kiro leans back against my cell door. "When Cari disappeared, Kleon told her he would return when she did. But my parents wanted to make sure there was nothing that would cause the other nations to lose faith in us."

"I know." I bit my lip, frustrated and impatient. All of this I already knew. "That's why I was ordered to pretend to be her."

"But before, once Toulacoeur was united under my ancestors' rule, slavery was abolished. Kleon denounced my mother when she agreed to make you her slave," Kiro explains softly.

Kiro tells me more—how Queen Arianna started to have panic attacks at the thought of the realms rising up against them, how she was so certain that Cari would return so soon. It is as if I can see my whole life pass before me, but now I see it differently. Suddenly it was seventeen years later, and I was still in her house as a slave, and Kleon's blessing had been removed from our family.

No. Kiro's family. Not mine.

My knees go weak.

"So now, if you run away with me, you'll no longer be a slave. And if you marry me, you'll be my wife," Kiro says. His cheeks flush over with a small amount of red, and at this, I soften my resolve. "I mean, if that is what you want."

Honestly, I don't know if Kiro is right about Kleon. But I trust Kiro, as I always have.

"Is that what you want?" I ask. My voice is barely audible, my mind still reeling with wonder.

"More than anything," Kiro says.

That is all I need to hear.

THE REALMS BEYOND THE RAINBOW

I run to him, and his arms open to embrace me. At once, I am enveloped in his warmth. His name escapes me in a rush of pleasure, and the moment I lift my face, his mouth is covering mine again.

I'd grown up with him, and now I want to grow old with him. If there is a way, I want to take it.

There is a quick knock at the dungeon door, and I am ungrateful for the distraction more than I am afraid of who might be on the other side.

I brighten to see Kiro is not scared at all. He opens the door and smiles. "There you are."

Juni is there. Her wrinkled face shows signs of sleeplessness, and I know from the careworn expression on her face she has been worried for me.

"Juni."

"Shh, Honeyspice." She shakes her head and curtsies before Kiro.

"I have finished everything you've requested of me, Highness," she whispers. "The horses are ready, and your bags are packed."

"Everything is going as planned. Good." Kiro grins at me as we begin to walk out of the castle hallways.

He beckons Juni to follow us, and she is already prepared to do so. Every so often, we see a guard, and Juni snaps her fingers.

THE REALMS BEYOND THE RAINBOW

"It's a code," Juni whispers to me as we head toward the stables. "The guards know not to look this way when they hear it, so they will not be able to testify later."

"I doubt they will get in trouble for letting Kiro do as he pleases," I say. There were countless times while we were growing up I'd seen him get away with plenty.

"Their Majesties are concerned for him, but they are more concerned with the kingdom," Juni says. "Right now, we are more concerned for you."

"Well, I certainly hope no one gets in trouble over me." I take her hand and squeeze it. "Promise me you'll be all right."

"There are more of us who are on your side then you realize." Juni pats my hand as we walk. "We've done our best to keep watch over you all these years. We have seen you take your punishments, and you have always acted in a gracious, honorable manner. After all we've watched you suffer, even though we did so little to help, we do love you."

"You do?"

"Of course we do," Kiro chimes in.

My heart almost aches for the king and queen; they must not know how many of their own servants—and their only son—are actively working against them, and all for my sake.

I pull her hand up to my lips and plant a kiss on her gnarled knuckles. "If there is ever anything I can do to repay you for your kindness, please do not hesitate to ask."

Juni's answer is quick and sure. "Keep us in your prayers while you are gone."

"I will do my best to reason with my parents from afar," Kiro promises.

Juni chuckles as we enter into the stables. Just as she said, there are two horses there, with packed bags mounted behind their saddles.

"As I said before your birthday celebration, Prince Kiro, it doesn't matter what you say to my Ari," Juni says. "She is afraid of the coming war. Both she and the king believe marriage with the Dovelion Warlords is the best way to negate it."

"They just might end up encouraging it," I say, recalling the fine armor and weapons of the Gryphon Riders.

"Sometimes preparing for war is the best way to avoid it," Kiro points out. "There's no real point in fighting a war you can't win."

"We might be in that situation soon," Juni says.

"I understand." Kiro bows his head to her, letting his chin rest on his chest. "I will extend my personal apologies to the Dovelion Warlords, and Ariella's father, for breaking off our engagement."

"She will never think it will be good enough, Prince Kiro."

"War is coming anyway, so long as Kitty is here," Kiro says.

Juni nods, and I blink. "You knew about that?" I ask.

"Ari's never hidden anything from me," Juni replies. "Not even her sins. I am bound by her power, but I answer a greater authority when it comes to loving you. I hope you know I did my best to protect you when I could, Honeyspice, even though it is a poor excuse."

"How long have you known?" I look over at Kiro and then at Juni, and the two of them exchange a knowing look.

"I found out last year, although it took me a few months to verify it," Kiro admits. "The queen had one of her spells and began to say all sorts of things, including how she just wanted to banish you."

"Banish me?"

"Yes." Kiro lifts me up onto one of the horses and hands me a dark, hooded cloak. "I couldn't object strongly enough, and when I forced her to tell me why, she told me the truth about you."

"She needs Cari," Juni says quietly, trying to soften the cruelty of my fate. "The kingdom needs Cari."

I say nothing as I tuck my legs into the sidesaddle. I don't know what to say to that. I could understand the reasons that the king and queen wanted to keep me around; without parents of my own, I don't have anyone else who will fight for me.

Except Kiro.

Kiro's eyes meet mine, and he reaches over, brushing a lock of my hair back behind my fox-cat ears. "Time to go, Kitty."

"Be safe," Juni says.

"Where are we going?" I ask.

Juni reaches up and tucks a scroll into my hand. "You'll be going to my brother's parish in the Shadowcaverns. He will be able to wed the two of you, and he will be able to provide you with a secure home."

I hesitate one last time; I am honor bound to serve the kingdom and its interests, and if I leave, I will be disobeying my rulers. But from what Kiro told me, I am not supposed to be a slave, and if I go with him, I will be more than free; I will be his wife, too.

"Are you sure?" I ask.

Kiro doesn't hesitate. "Yes."

Juni beams with joy. "Be safe, my children."

"Thank you." Kiro leans down and kisses Juni's cheek affectionately. "I knew if I could count on anyone, it would be you."

THE REALMS BEYOND THE RAINBOW

"Oh, shush now, Highness. Just promise me you'll take care of my Honeyspice."

"I'll take care of her. But she's mine now."

"Aren't you always such a charmer," Juni mutters. "You've always been good to her, though, so I have no reason to doubt you now. I can trust you, Prince Kiro."

"Just as I can trust you to see to my mother's care," Kiro replies.

Juni nods solemnly. "I'll see to her now," she says. "I can buy you some more time that way. Ari has never been the same since Cari."

She says her last goodbyes to us, and for just a quick, lingering moment, I want to stay with her. Juni is the closest thing I have to a mother. But I already know what she will say to me if I hesitate, and from her love and the love of others, I find the courage and strength to leave.

Kiro and I snap our horses' reins, and we head out of the castle.

The peace I felt before returns, and I no longer wish to look back.

THE REALMS BEYOND THE RAINBOW

CHAPTER SIX

It is not until the forest is far behind us that I truly take what I consider to be my first breath of freedom.

It tastes too much like fear for me to be excited. I cough as I inhale. When Kiro looks at me and laughs a second later, I soon find myself laughing along with him.

"It's not that different from palace life," Kiro says.

"So you say," I retort.

"This is just one of our secret adventures, Kitty." Kiro slows down his horse, allowing me to come up beside him. "We've got a plan, right? Everything will be fine."

Our hands come together, grasping at each other, and I smile. If this is one of our secret adventures, it is the adventure of our lifetime. So many before had been sneaking out to the castle kitchens or heading into Auralis without an escort.

"I do love you," I whisper, and Kiro squeezes my hand. "I hope you're right."

Kiro pulls us to a stop, long enough to cup my chin and bring me close enough for a kiss.

Just as our lips touch, a gong sounds out all around us, loud enough the horses fret.

"Kiro," I whisper. "They know you're missing."

Beside me, Kiro says nothing. He frowns as he glances back toward the kingdom.

"I don't know if that's it," he says. "That's not the right signal. It would be different."

"What else could it be?"

There is a small explosion just ahead to the far right of us, and I look up to see a strange burst of light coming up from the woods. I grab my ears at the noise, even as I am dazzled by the array of lights.

A flower of fire lights up the sky, before smoking out into nothing.

As I look at the stars above, and as the flare in the sky disappears into smoke, I remember the shooting star we'd seen the night before.

"Kiro," I say. "This is close to where the shooting star would've landed, isn't it?"

Kiro looks back and forth, and finally nods in agreement. "You're right," he says. "I've never heard of an exploding meteor, though."

"Let's go see it," I say. Now that I am free, even the possible danger of the situation doesn't frighten

THE REALMS BEYOND THE RAINBOW

me as much. I spur my horse forward, and Kiro follows me.

I stop short at the sight before me.

"Lights above," I whisper, my voice echoing with incredulity.

There is a unicorn standing before me. He is barely taller than my own horse, with his coat of the purest white. His mane sparkles with the dust of starlight, and his eyes are a deep, eternal blend of color and time. There is a horn in the middle of his forehead that glimmers, and just underneath it is a red diamond, matching the size of the ruby from Princess Cari's crown. I blink, and at the dryness in my eyes, I realize I have been staring, wide-eyed, at the Unicorn who guards all of Toulacoeur.

Behind me, Kiro speaks. "Kleon."

Kleon paws the ground with one of his hooves, before he comes up beside us. He nods at Kiro, and then his eyes meet mine.

Time, along with the rest of the world, goes still.

Kleon doesn't move his mouth, but I hear a voice inside my head.

"Kitsuneko."

I quickly duck my head at once in a hurried curtsy, profusely apologetic for my rudeness.

I can almost hear his chuckle as he speaks to me again.

THE REALMS BEYOND THE RAINBOW

"There is no reason to fear me, Kitsuneko. After all your time in the castle, you have proven yourself to be an honorable woman, whose loyalty and faithfulness are the rarest gems to be found."

My eyes are suddenly wet with tears again. "Thank you, Lord Kleon."

"There is no need to call me 'Lord,' but instead, I ask you call me 'Friend.' For all your suffering at the hands of my Keeper, I will grant you and your prince safe passage to the Shadowcaverns, along with my deepest apologies and with my sincerest blessing for your marriage. Go, and be well. You will see me again before too long."

Kleon turns away from me, and the moment is broken. I can feel time moving again; I can hear Kiro's breathing and sense the jitters from the horses. I can even smell the faintest tinge of smoke in the air, coming from where the brightly colored flare had exploded.

"Where do you think he's headed?" Kiro asks as we watch Kleon's tail flicker and then disappear into the woods.

"I don't know," I reply. "But he told me—"

"He spoke to you?"

"You didn't hear him?" I grip my hands tightly on my horse's reins. "He said he was sorry for what the queen had done to me, but he would make sure we were safe as we made it to the Shadowcaverns. Do you think he's going there, too?"

THE REALMS BEYOND THE RAINBOW

"I doubt it." Kiro comes up beside me on his horse. "But if he's back, maybe that means Cari is, too."

"Do you really think so?" I glance toward the castle. "Maybe we should return to Auralis."

"If Kleon gave us the blessing of safe passage to the Shadowcaverns, we should take it," Kiro says. "He is the guardian of this world, and the one who speaks for God."

"That's right," I say. This time my voice is hushed, full of awe.

I don't know why it has taken me so long to see it, but I know now that my prayers have been answered, and they have been answered in ways I could never have imagined.

For a long moment, my head falls into my hands; this time, not in despair, but in disbelief. "I don't believe this. I don't deserve this. This is all too much."

Kiro pries my hands away from me. "Oh, Kitty," he whispers, toying with my fox-cat ears and tracing the white marks that surround my eyes. "You haven't even begun to see what good things lie ahead of us."

Then he reaches over and kisses me again. As his mouth moves over mine, I wrap my arms around Kiro's neck and sigh happily.

I am alive, I am free, and it is all wonder to me that I am loved.

THE REALMS BEYOND THE RAINBOW

Kiro gently pulls away from me. "Are you ready to go?"

"Yes." There is no more doubt inside of me as we ride on toward our future together.

AUTHOR'S NOTE

Dear Reader,

My profoundest apologies are due you at the moment of this writing. It seems as with all of my life, I am having trouble focusing on one particular series at a time. But this story came to me as a rainbow during one of my bouts of depression and anxiety, and I liked it enough I wanted to keep it, and as I began to write it, I fell ever more deeply in love with it. I like to think this is to your benefit as well as mine, as there are several of you who have been asking me to write more fantasy again, and so, here we are. God certainly does grant us his goodness in all things.

I have been toying with a rainbow portal series idea for a while now. As I watch my children, I love to see their eyes widen and their smiles grow, and recently, they have been enjoying a good dose of space books and places. They enjoy playing astronauts and my own little girl has always been my princess; so in writing this story, I am writing it for her and for our time together in contemplating the grand things of creation.

For this book, I also must credit my friend Laura. The best people I know are the ones who seem to dream clearly, and Laura's idea to embark on being a manga writer is one that has me cheering. As several of her friends and I were discussing names for her manga print, I suggested "Kitsuneko," which is a

THE REALMS BEYOND THE RAINBOW

portmanteau of the Japanese words "kitsune," or a fox demon, and "neko," which is cat. After I said it, I wanted to keep it.

I wanted to keep it and write a story to go with it.

So here we are, and this is indeed a place of blessing where we're at—so many layers of blessing in this place, too, as Princess Cari's return to Toulacoeur will be further explored in the next book, *Return of the Lost Princess,* Book One of The Realms Beyond the Rainbow.

I hope to see you there! In the meantime, if you're one of my fantasy loving fans, please read on for a sample chapter of my original fairy tale, *The Princess and the Peacock,* the first in my Birds of Fae series.

Until We Meet Again,

C. S. Johnson

C. S. JOHNSON

Chapter 1

from

THE

Princess

AND THE

BIRDS OF FAE

BOOK 1

THE REALMS BEYOND THE RAINBOW

C. S. JOHNSON

THE REALMS BEYOND THE RAINBOW

1

◊

The first time I fell in love with Princess Mele was when I saw her smile, and I fell in love with her the second time the moment I heard her sing.

The memory of the day I met her is burned into my mind as much as the scars of my mother's death have been scorched on my hands—my hands, which are currently full of cuts and scrapes as I make my way up the Forbidden Mountain.

Its steep climb and deep crevices make for easier climbing than it first appears, but there have been enough deaths in my village that no one has tried to climb it for several summers now. The last warrior to go up the mountain went during the summer of my seventeenth year. After he fell, he was left to die at the foot of the mountain, his body broken and his eyes blinded.

I know all of this because I am the one who found him, and Appa was the one who took him in and nursed him back to health.

The man was saved from death, but not from disgrace. It was thought to be bad luck to touch a blind man in my village. His family reluctantly took him in, and they were relieved he died shortly after, no matter how glorious a warrior he had once been.

No one wants to care for an outcast.

My eyes fall to my scars on my hands, the ones that wind their way up the left side of my body, curving all around my arms, and dipping down across my back.

No one wants to be associated with one, either.

I know that truth as much as I know the pain associated with my own dismissal from the ranks of my fellow warriors after my disfigurement.

My fingers slip on a rock as it breaks free from the rest of the mountain. I hurry, reaching for another one before I lose my grip completely. I clasp onto another divot in the mountain and slowly release my breath in staggered pants. Even if I am no longer a soldier for my kingdom, and I've lost some of my stamina since my mother's death, I still have plenty of strength from my years of training.

The blood on my palms is sticky and hot, compelling me onward and upward, but I know I should take a moment to rest, to allow my heart to slowly beat back to its normal pattern.

Resting does not appeal to me, even though I have been climbing for hours now; I do not want the opportunity to focus on my pain, nor do I want to dwell on the ugliness that brands me as an outcast in my village. I only want to remember the moment Princess Mele entered my world. She came into my world, offering it the only possible hope for meaning and giving me the only reason I had to move forward with my life after the death of my mother.

It might have been two years since I fell in love with her, but not a night has gone by since then that I have not dreamed of her. And now that King Ahanu, her father, is ready to see her wed, I have to do something quickly if I am to earn her hand in marriage.

So I need to do this, I tell myself. No matter how hard it is, I need to climb up the Forbidden Mountain.

THE REALMS BEYOND THE RAINBOW

Remembering her beauty is the only way I will make it to the top of the mountain, the only way I can ever hope to gain beauty of my own. And that means forgetting my pain, no matter how well I am accustomed to it.

"Kaipo, wait up."

As I hear my name, I groan and nearly stumble again.

Rahj is calling for me.

I struggle to secure myself once more, torn between irritation and relief. I pull back from the mountain, very, very carefully, enough to where I can peek through the crook of my elbow. More than twenty *guz* below me, my best and only friend is faithfully following me.

Reluctantly, I settle further into the mountain crevice where I've stopped, deciding it is better for Rahj to catch up to me.

That is the big secret of success when it comes to climbing the Forbidden Mountain—it is much easier to climb if someone else is around to help. No one else ever seemed to realize that before.

But then, there was a reward at stake. If a climber wanted to earn a wish from Jaya, the Fae Queen residing at the peak, he had to survive the climb to see her. In all the centuries since our kingdom's founders settled on the isle of Maluhia, only a few warriors have ever completed the task.

I look up, squinting past the longer strands of my ash brown hair to gaze at the majestic mountain as its peak disappears into the lofty clouds. Even on clear days, no one ever sees the crown of the mountain; it is well-known that Jaya likes her privacy, and with all her birds and magic for company, she never willingly bothers the mortals residing on her island.

"I'm coming, Kaipo. You sure are a fast climber!" The chill in the high mountain allows his voice to move more swiftly through the air between us.

I watch as Rahj draws closer to me. Out of the corner of my eye, I can see the tunic he is wearing; it is one of my older ones, one of the few we had been able to save from the fire. It strikes a stark contrast with the brightness around it, but the charcoal dye manages to hide a good deal of tears and dirt. My own tunic is better repaired, but the lighter tan coloring brings out the whiteness of my scars.

I lean back and look over at him as he climbs. "Are you doing well, Rahj?" I ask, already knowing the answer he will give.

Rahj comes up beside me, the usual grin on his face. "Of course I am well, brother."

I never know why he is so happy. I try not to let his persistent cheerfulness bother me as we continue our climb up the mountain.

I used to hate Rahj, and I remember this on occasions such as this one. It has been seven years since he came to live with us after Appa saved his life.

To this day, I do not know the full story of how it happened; I only knew Rahj was a former child slave from the neighboring island of Aruna, one of the of many boys castrated in service to the temple goddesses. My father had gone to Aruna in hopes of trading some of his herbal mixtures for some supplies.

THE REALMS BEYOND THE RAINBOW

But instead of new tools or perhaps even some of the exotic candies from the West my friends' fathers purchased, my father bought Rahj, using all his coins and trading the last of his medicines to do so.

It seemed my father's action would doom us all, especially when Appa told us he'd brought Rahj home to live with us, not as a slave, but as an adopted son. Several members of my family, including my mother, grew suspicious of the strange boy suddenly part of our family; with his ochre skin and his reddish hair, many assumed Rahj was my father's bastard, born to him by an Arunian temple prostitute.

The whispers only got worse as my mother rejected my father and refused to see him again so long as he was alive.

From that day on, my mother had taken to her bed, always insisting she was ill. When I asked her about it, as young as I was, she insisted that something had to be wrong with her, that she had only been able to have one son, and that Appa still felt the need to buy his own.

"Something is probably wrong with you, too, Kaipo," she'd muttered, before shoving me away and pulling her blanket over her head. I never saw her move from her bed after that, not even when Appa died, just shy of my eighteenth year.

At the thought of my mother, and picturing her sad and crying as she burned herself to death, I look down at my hands. They are currently full of blood and dirt, the stinging mixture serving as an adhesive between me and the side of the mountain I am climbing.

The pain I'd pushed back earlier refuses to be ignored any longer. The vicious rawness courses through my body, roaming from the tips of my bloody fingers to the center of my heart, before flying up and anchoring itself into my mind. The alarm I feel sends tremors down my body, and I squeeze my eyes shut and force myself to keep going.

The rocks continue to rip into my palms as I climb, but I use the thought of Princess Mele to ward off the pain, just like I used to keep her memory close at night, when I would worry bad dreams would come to me after my mother died.

One side of my mouth quirks up in an involuntary smile; the idea of remaining calm while hanging onto the side of a mountain—let alone the Forbidden Mountain, the home of the Fae Queen, Jaya—is laughable.

"Hey, Kaipo, we are almost at the top!" Rahj lets out a cheer as he appears beside me again. He daringly loosens his grip before twisting around to see the sights behind us. "Can you believe the view from up here? No wonder Jaya chose to live here."

I carefully look down at the view below. I can see our whole side of Maluhia as I glance around us. The skies are clear, shining in a way that seems both too light and too blue; the clouds just above the Forbidden Mountain are fluffy and starkly white, as if they know they are used in service to a higher power.

The seas that surround Maluhia are a mix of blue and green, the sun and sky eagerly battling for the right to blend their beauty. I can see the coral reef that bends around the beach that leads to the other side of the mountain, where the kingdom's rich merchants, warriors, and royal family live in the capital city of Shanthi.

"You're right," I say to Rahj, who somehow smiles even more brightly. "This is incredible."

THE REALMS BEYOND THE RAINBOW

"This is how the God of all creation must see the world," Rahj says, his voice full of awe. "From up here, it only looks beautiful. There is no way to see the full ugliness the world carries."

I frown at him, surprised by the remark. There was nothing in his tone to suggest a sullen feeling, but the words were enough to make me wonder.

"I am happy to share this with you, Kaipo." Despite the danger, Rahj reaches out and I clasp his hand in mine.

I might have hated Rahj before, but since my scars had branded me as both an outcast and an orphan, he had remained by my side. With Appa gone, and my mother dead and burned, there is no one else.

So I smile at him. "Thank you, brother," I reply, and this time, Rahj does not smile. Instead, I can see the solemn gratitude and pride in his gaze as he nods.

His sudden and uncharacteristic seriousness is the last thing I see before the rock under his anchored hand crumbles, and he cries out my name as he falls.

"Kaipo!"

Thank you for reading! Please leave a review for this book and check out www.csjohnson.me for other books and updates!

THE REALMS BEYOND THE RAINBOW